Contents

Basic perspective

Any composition can become more interesting and dramatic by the use of extreme or 'forced' perspective. This eye-catching approach is often used in advertising and for film posters. Start experimenting by drawing your subject at close range so that the angles and shapes become more exaggerated. This will create a punchier look to any image.

The vanishing point (V.P.) is the place in a perspective drawing where parallel lines appear to meet. The position of the vanishing point depends on the viewer's eye level.

The Spinnaker Tower in Portsmouth

Low eye-level (view from below): sometimes a low viewpoint can give your drawing added drama.

HOW TO DRAW™ EXTREME PERSPECTIVE

Mark Bergin

BOOK  HOUSE

SALARIYA

Published in Great Britain in MMXVI by
Book House, an imprint of
The Salariya Book Company Ltd
25 Marlborough Place, Brighton BN1 1UB

1 3 5 7 9 8 6 4 2

Author: Mark Bergin was born in Hastings in 1961. He studied at Eastbourne College of Art and has specialised in historical reconstructions as well as aviation and maritime subjects since 1983. He lives in Bexhill-on-Sea with his wife and three children.

Editor: Nick Pierce

PB ISBN: 978-1-910706-55-8

A CIP catalogue record for this book is available from the British Library.

Printed and bound in China.
Printed on paper from sustainable sources.

WARNING: Fixatives should be used only under adult supervision.

Visit our websites to read interactive **free** web books, stay up to date with new releases, catch up with us on the Book House Blog, view our electronic catalogue and more!

www.salariya.com
Free electronic versions of four of our *You Wouldn't Want to Be* titles

www.book-house.co.uk
Online catalogue
Information books
and graphic novels

www.scribobooks.com
Fiction books

www.scribblersbooks.com
Books for babies, toddlers and pre-school children

www.flickr.com/photos/salariyabookhouse
View our photostream with sneak previews of forthcoming titles

Join the conversation on Facebook and Twitter by visiting
www.salariya.com

Visit our YouTube channel to see Mark Bergin doing step by step illustrations:
www.youtube.com/user/BookHouse100

Visit
www.salariya.com
for our online catalogue and
free interactive web books.

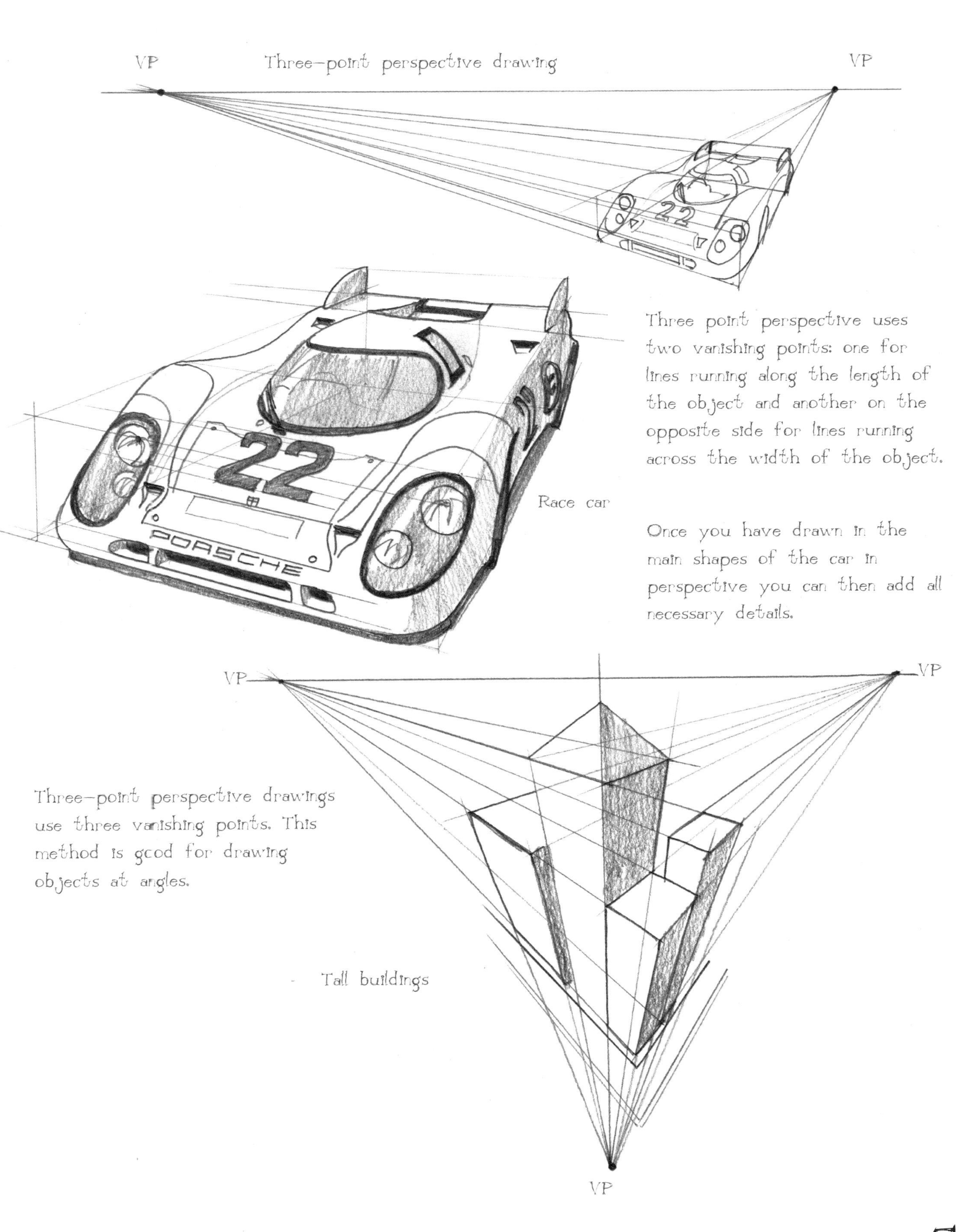
VP
Three-point perspective drawing
VP
Three point perspective uses two vanishing points: one for lines running along the length of the object and another on the opposite side for lines running across the width of the object.
22
PORSCHE
Race car
Once you have drawn in the main shapes of the car in perspective you can then add all necessary details.
VP
VP
Three-point perspective drawings use three vanishing points. This method is good for drawing objects at angles.
Tall buildings
VP

Drawing materials

Once you've chosen your subject, decide which medium will best depict it. Try using different types of drawing papers and materials. Experiment with charcoal, wax crayons and pastels. All pens, from felt-tips to ballpoints, will make interesting marks, or try drawing with pen and ink on wet paper.

Silhouette is a style of drawing that shows only a solid black shape.

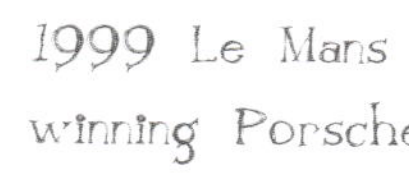

1999 Le Mans winning Porsche

Coloured pencils are soft and easily smudged. Use fixative to protect the drawing.

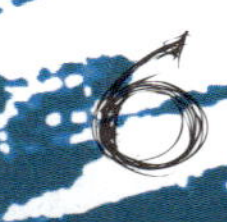

Experiment with different grades of **pencil** to maximise the range of light and shade in your drawing. Hard pencils are grayer and soft pencils are blacker. Hard pencils usually range from 6H (the hardest) to 5H, 4H, 3H, 2H and H. Soft pencils are graded from B, 2B, 3B, 4B and 5B up to 6B (the softest). HB is between H and B.

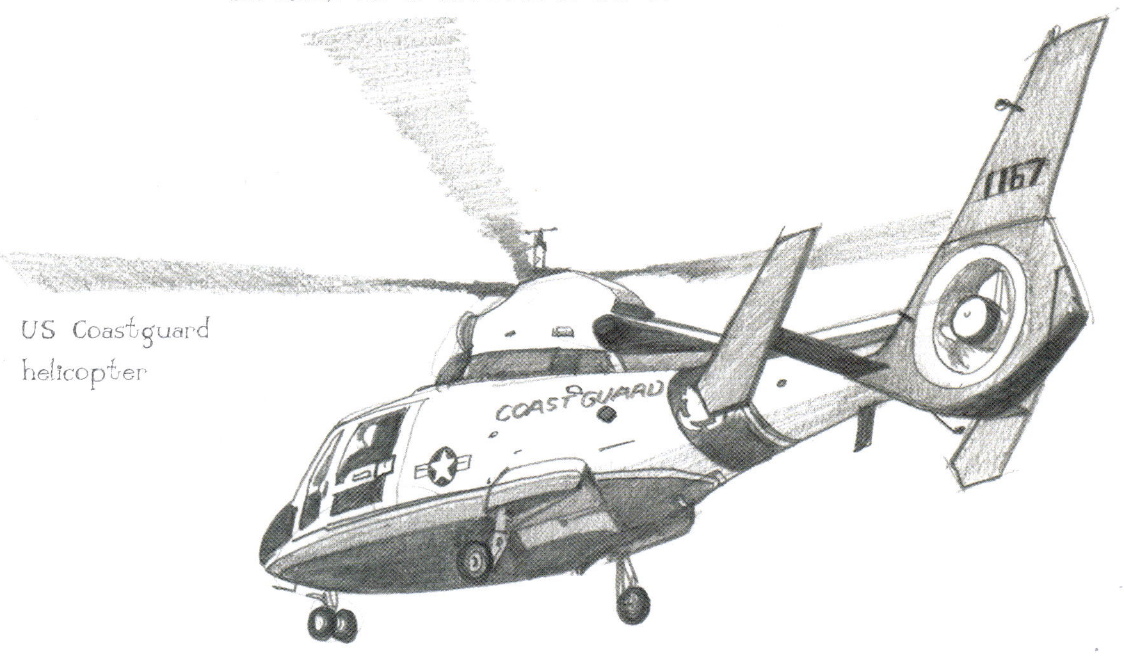

US Coastguard helicopter

Lines drawn in **ink** cannot be erased, so keep your ink drawings sketchy and less rigid. Don't worry about mistakes as these lines can be lost in the drawing as it develops.

Wrecked boat

Using photos

Drawing from photographs is a helpful way to tackle subjects or locations that are not easily accessed. Photographs also make it much easier to study and draw a subject in motion.

First choose a good photograph and trace it. Then draw a grid of squares over the tracing. Now draw a faint grid of the same proportions onto your drawing paper. Copy the shapes from each square of the tracing onto the drawing-paper grid.

When drawing, remember to keep your viewpoint consistent.

Once the outline is complete, start adding more details to the drawing. Always refer back to the grid for accuracy.

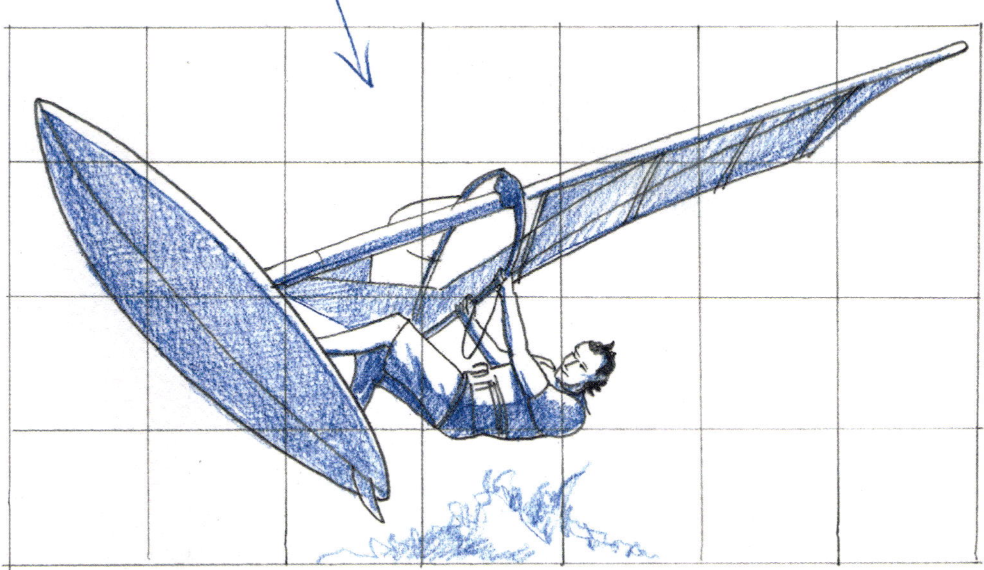

Now add form to your drawing. Decide on a light source and add shading to the parts of the drawing where light would not reach.

Use hatching and cross-hatching to enhance the three-dimensional effect.

Street scene

Three-point perspective is used when the viewpoint is either very low or very high. An aerial or ground-level photo of skyscrapers creates a dramatic viewpoint.

When you look up at an object, the vanishing point will be above your eye level.

Low eye-level (view from below)

In this high-level view the buildings' lines dramatically converge towards a low vanishing point. The rooftops of the buildings will also be visible.

High eye-level (view from above)

The vanishing point will be below your eye level. It may even be below ground level.

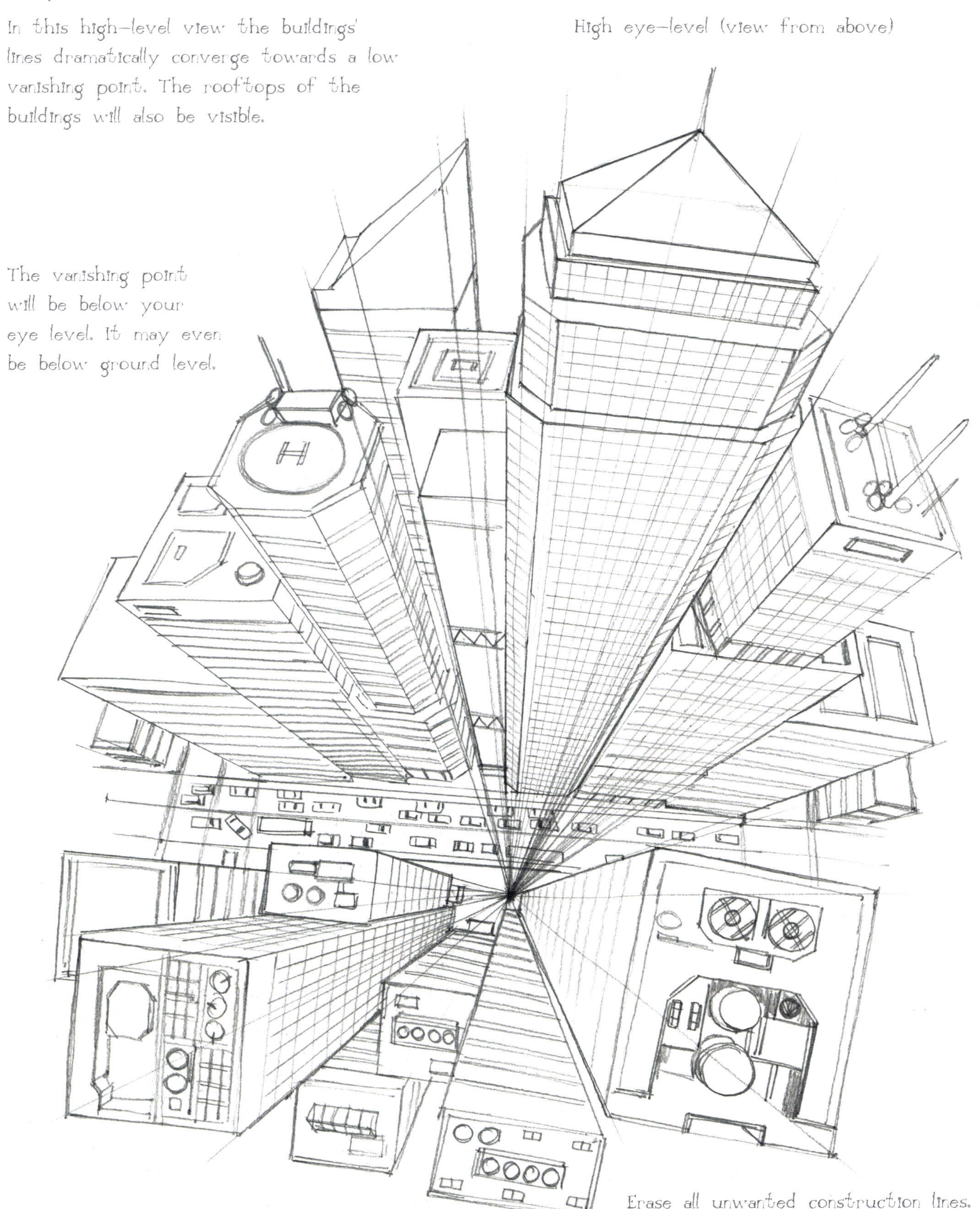

Erase all unwanted construction lines.

Buildings in the round

This type of extreme perspective mimics the photographic effect of a fish-eye lens. It produces strong visual distortion that creates a wide panoramic image. It's an ideal format to present cityscapes and landscapes in a dynamic, striking way.

This vanishing point is at the centre of the circle.

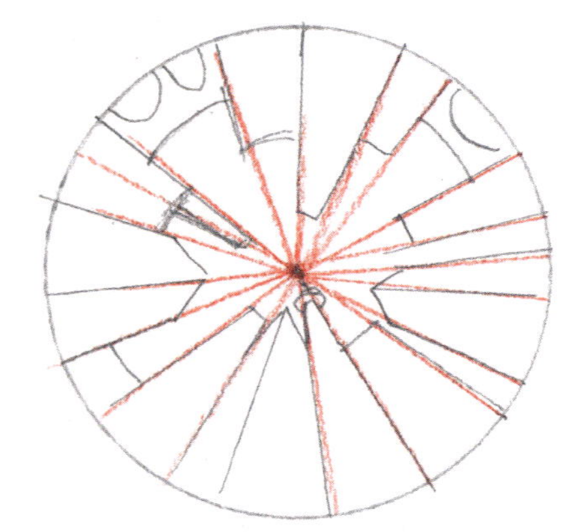

This circular image contains landmarks found in the city of London.

This extreme perspective image shows a fanciful city formed of many of the world's most famous architectural landmarks.

Every building or landmark shares the same central V.P. Overlapping images create added interest.

Erase all unwanted construction lines.

Fantasy castles

Extreme perspective is a good device for conveying extraordinary scale and dimensions. For this reason it lends itself to drawing subjects that are fantastical, such as these fairytale castles.

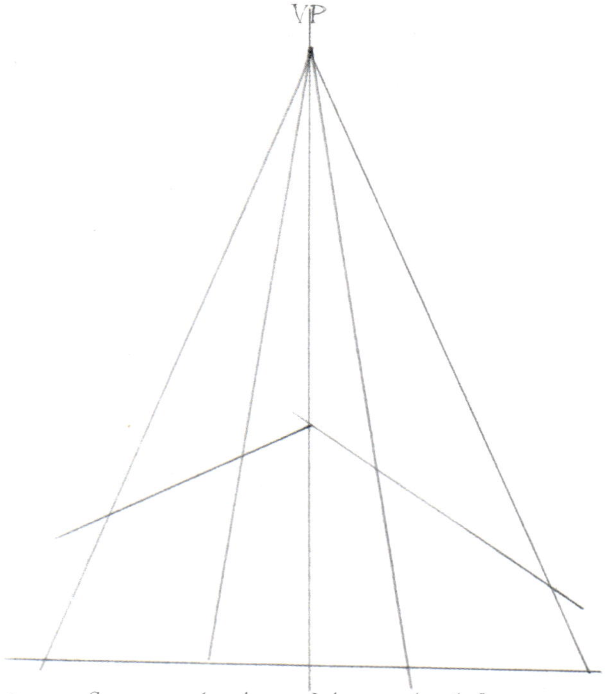

VP

Start to sketch in the outline of the castle, including its turrets and drawbridge.

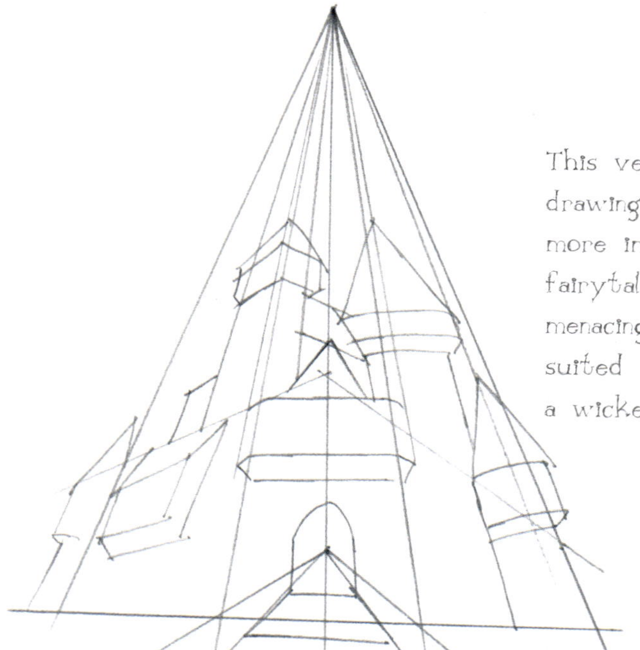

Draw five vertical guidelines stretching towards the vanishing point at the top.

Fill in the finer details of the castle and the mountain it's sitting atop.

This very low-eye-level drawing makes the castle look more imposing and sinister. The fairytale element now looks menacing. This approach might be suited to drawing the castle of a wicked queen or wizard.

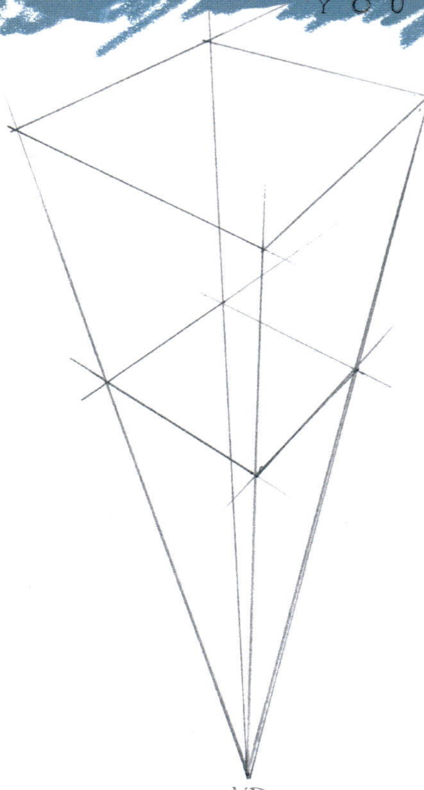

Draw a cube as seen from above and four guidelines stretching from it to the vanishing point below.

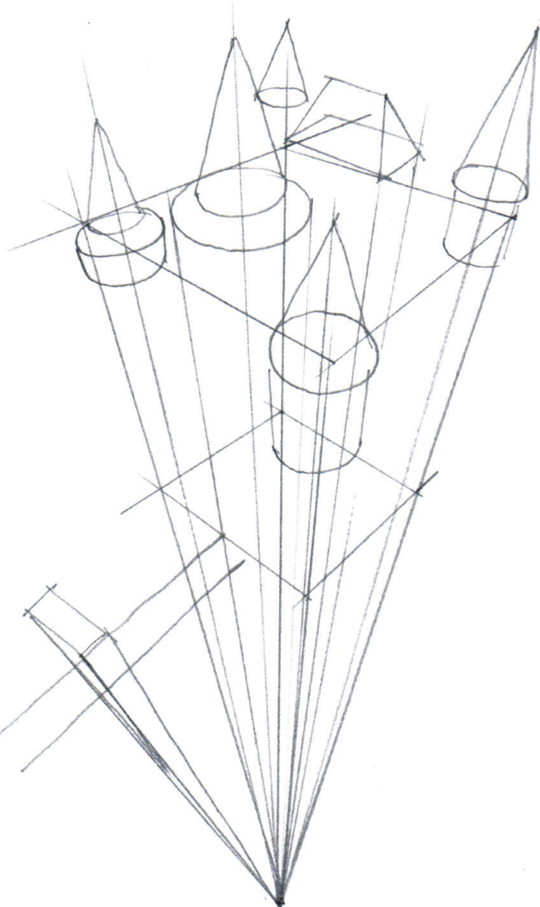

Draw in the turrets on the top of the castle and the basic outline of the drawbridge leading up to it.

Fill in the architectural details on the outside of the castle, as well as the surrounding landscape and the horseman riding up the drawbridge.

This bird's-eye view of the castle emphasises its impregnable size in relation to its surroundings. It makes an effective viewpoint for a princess to be imprisoned or cut off from the outside world.

Erase all unwanted construction lines.

Human body foreshortening

The use of foreshortening in a drawing is an optical illusion to create a sense of three-dimensional space. An understanding of perspective is vital to this technique. The subject is drawn so that those parts closest to the viewer appear larger.

Foreshortened hand

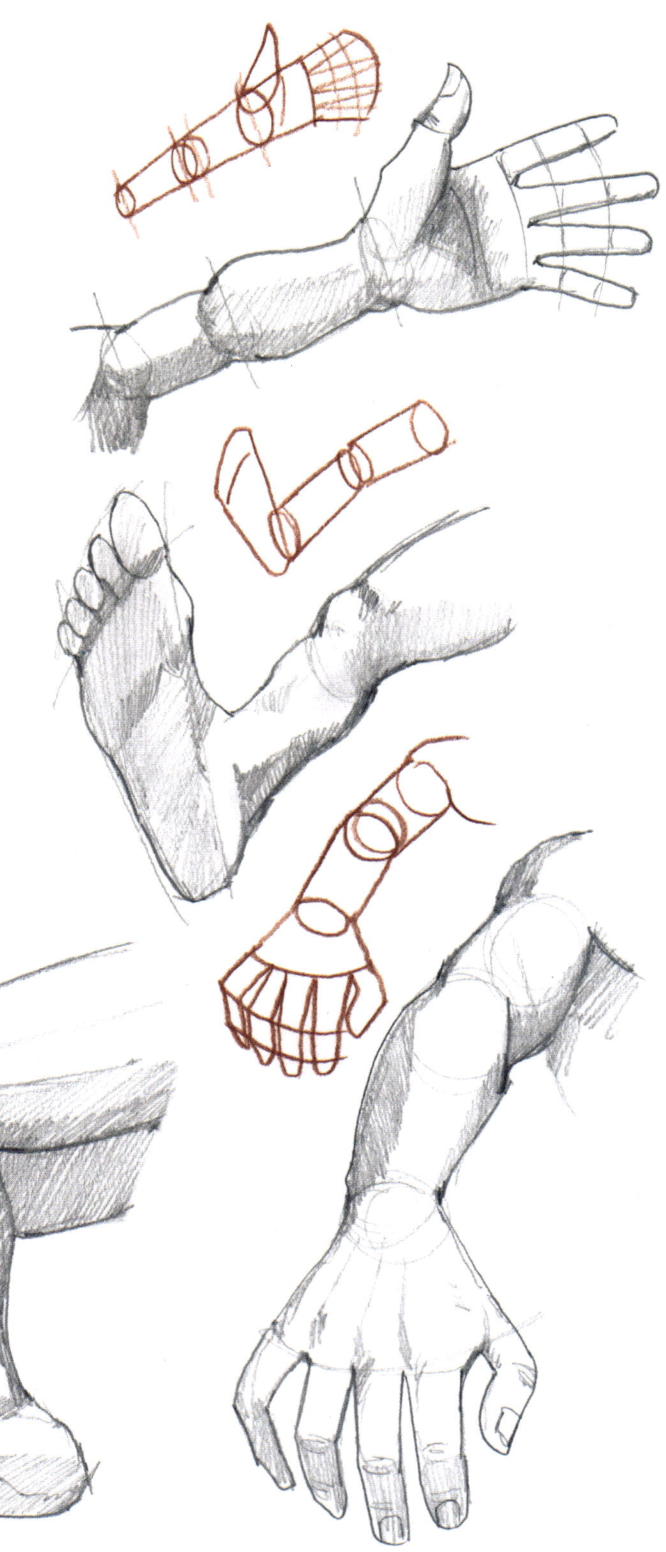

Foreshortened feet

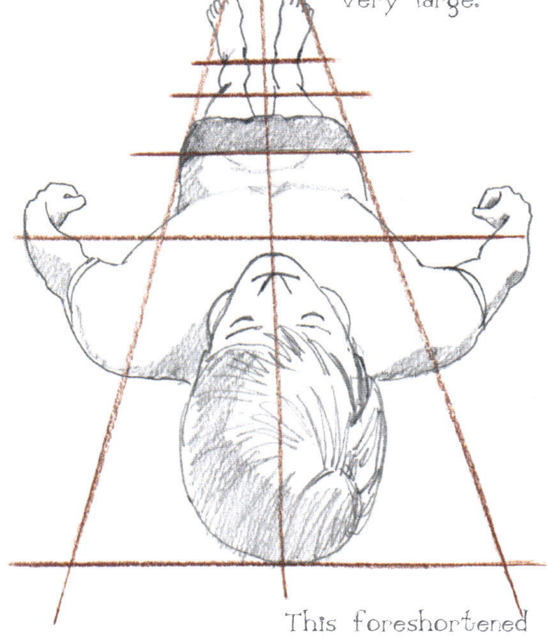

This foreshortened high-angle drawing makes the figure's feet seem very small and his head very large.

This foreshortened high-angle drawing makes the ballerina's feet seem very small and her raised arm very large.

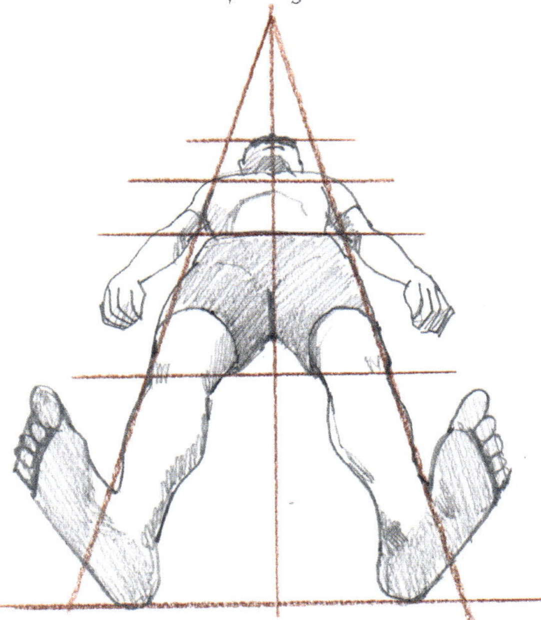

This foreshortened low-angle drawing reverses the effect: the figure's feet seem very large and his head very small.

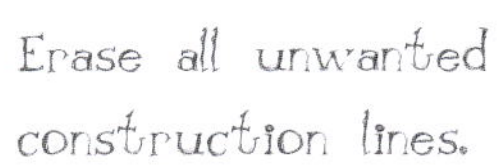

Erase all unwanted construction lines.

Human body in motion

Perspective is vitally important when drawing the figure in motion. Try to keep your construction lines more fluid to capture a sense of movement. Angling figures towards or away from the viewer can help to emphasise the force, direction or dynamism of the movement depicted.

Practise drawing quick sketches of a wide variety of poses.

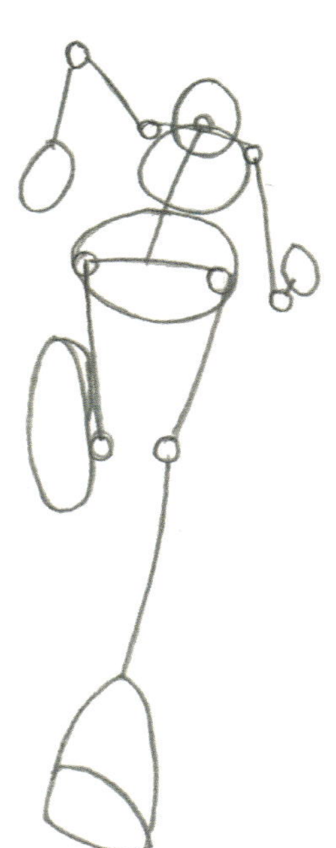

Jogging

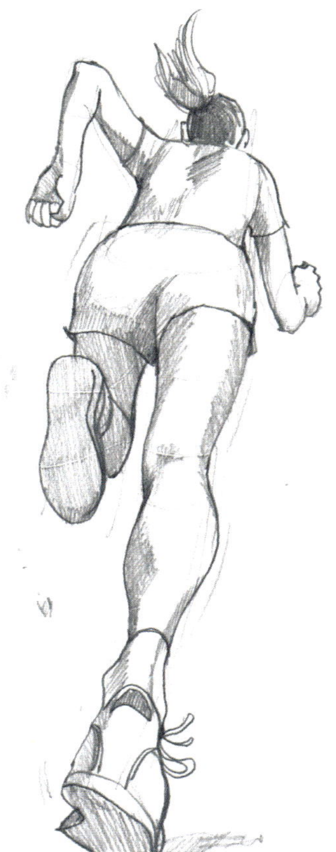

Archery

Study the shapes made by people in action. Try to get a strong sense of movement into your drawing.

Martial arts

Surfing

Erase all unwanted consruction lines.

Extreme sports

The use of perspective can create a strong feeling of space in your drawing. This is ideal for drawing extreme sports, where the surrounding location can play a big part in conveying a sense of speed and movement through space.

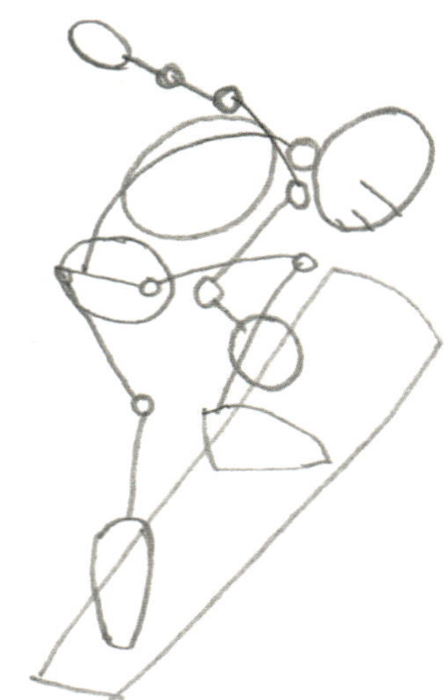

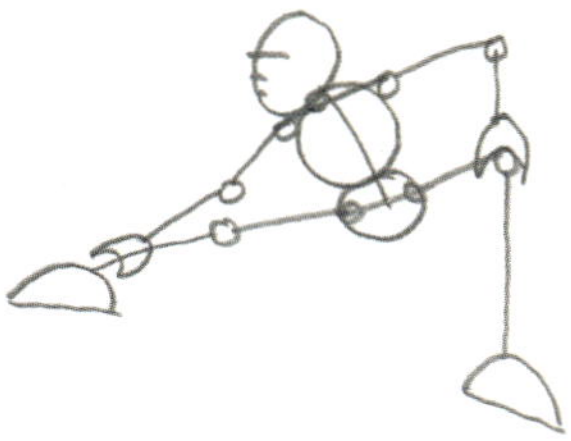

Snowboarding

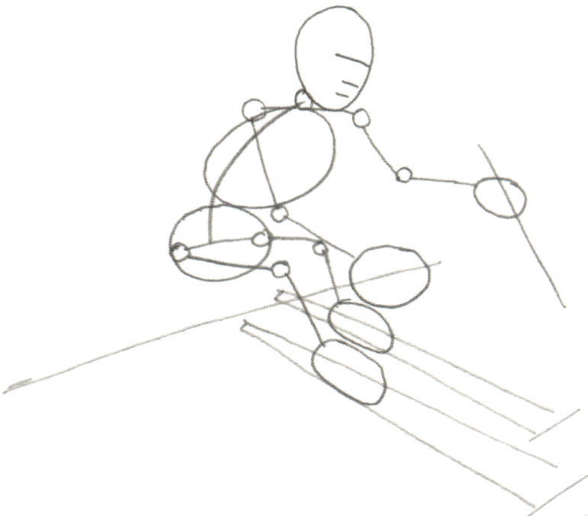

Skiing

Free running

Study and practise drawing the shapes made by people participating in a wide variety of extreme sports. Try to get a strong sense of movement into your drawing.

Composition

Composition is the arrangement of the picture, or the various parts of the picture, on the paper. Does your drawing look better in an upright (portrait) format or as a horizontal (landscape) format?

Erase all unwanted consruction lines.

Extreme animals

Extreme perspective can be used to good effect to show the extraordinary physical traits of different animal species.

Start by drawing a basic stick-figure outline of the giraffe, including the various joints in its legs.

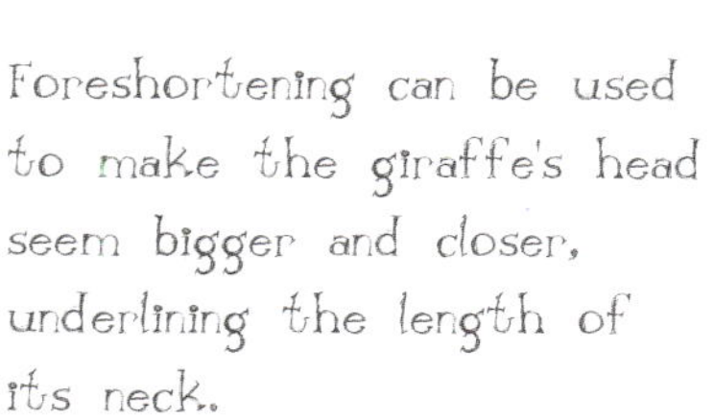

Foreshortening can be used to make the giraffe's head seem bigger and closer, underlining the length of its neck.

Giraffe

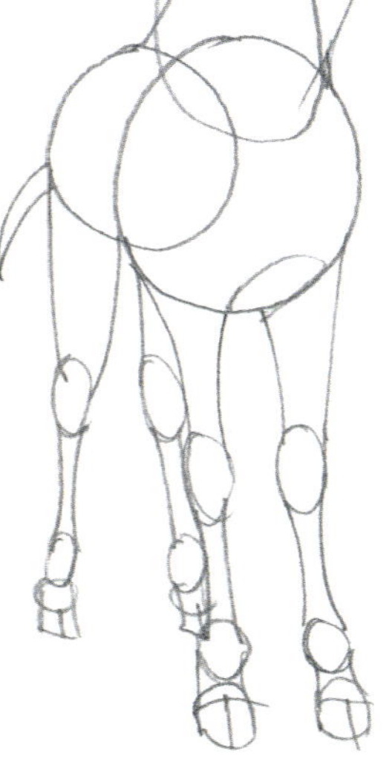

Add further details to the giraffe, including its hooves, facial features and tail.

Use shading to create the texture and patterning on the giraffe's body, as well as the shadow it casts.

Draw the basic outlines of the dolphin's curving body, flippers and jaws.

Add the dolphin's eye, tail and back fins, and its blowhole.

Use shading to give the dolphin its distinctive silver-grey body and paler underside.

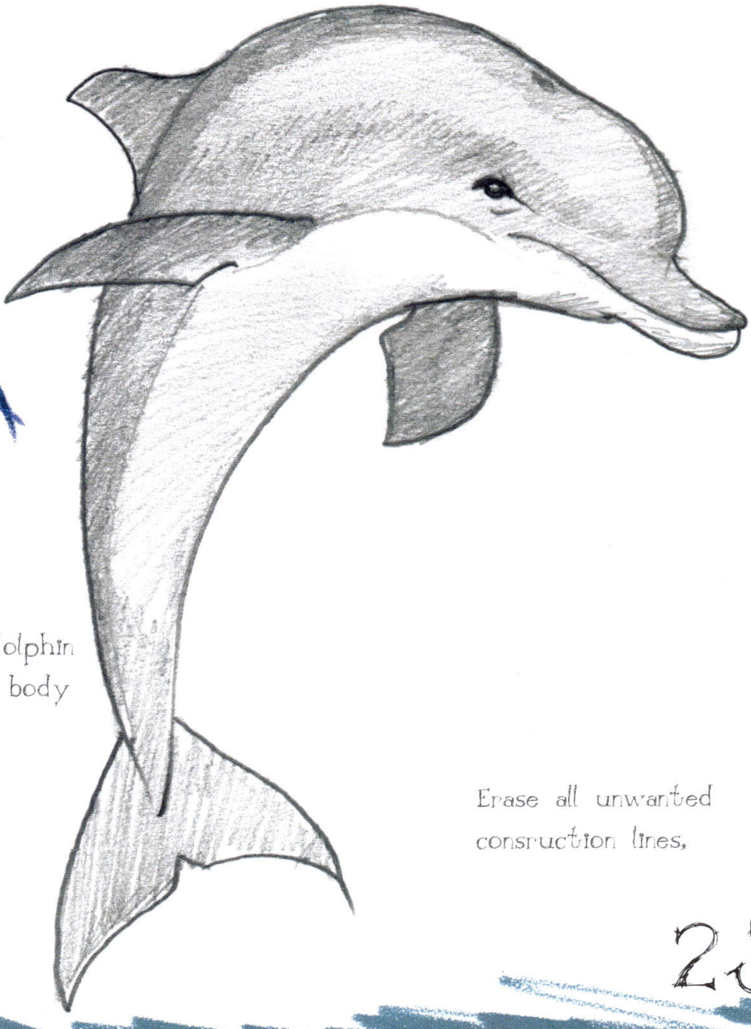

Erase all unwanted consruction lines.

Extreme cars

If you look at a car from different viewpoints, you will see that the part that is closest to you will always look larger, and the part furthest away from you will look smaller. Drawing cars in perspective creates a dynamic three-dimensional image on paper.

Mercedes F1 car, 2015

The lines converge towards the V.P. so that the front of the car appears much wider and bigger than the rear.

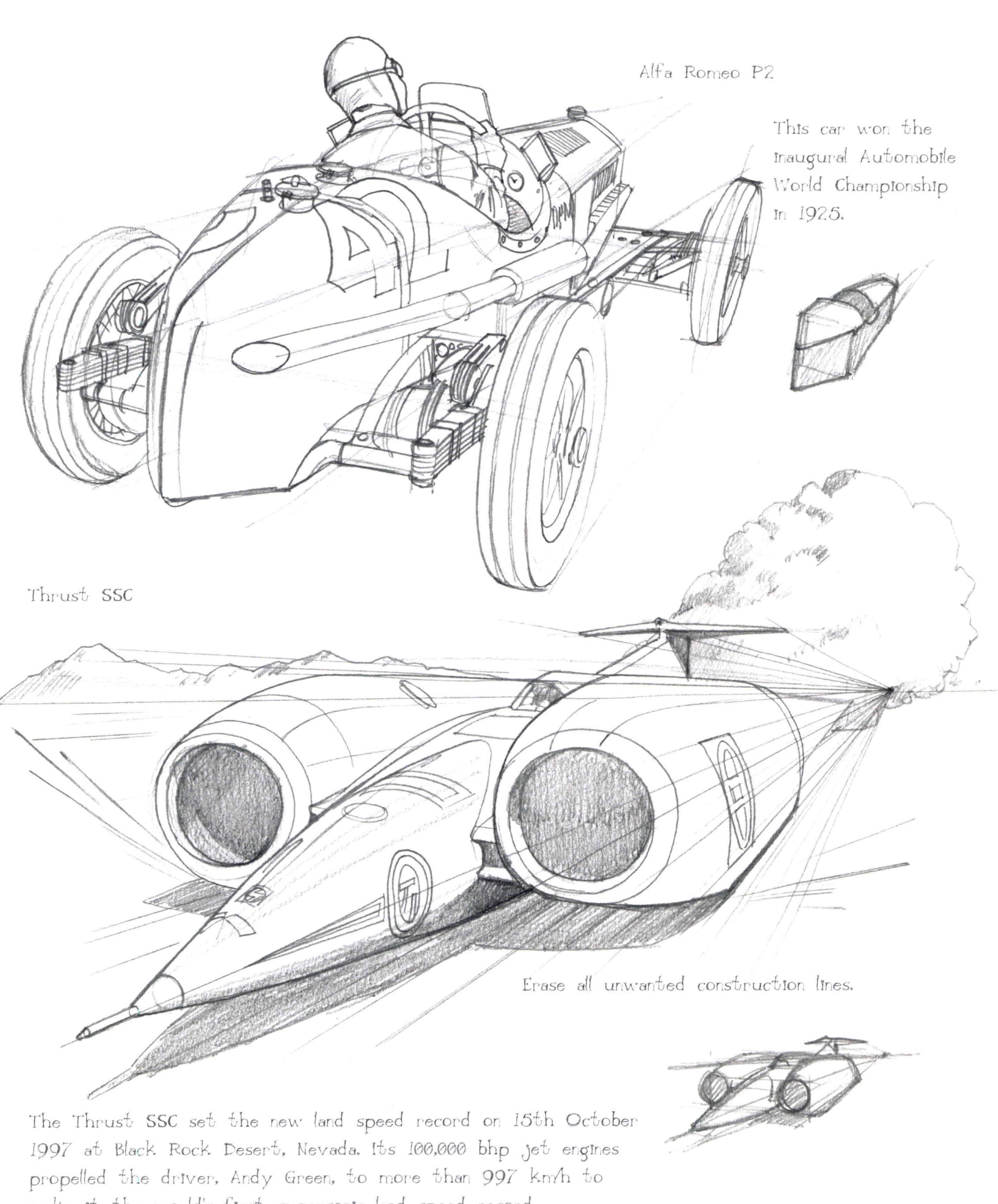

The Thrust SSC set the new land speed record on 15th October 1997 at Black Rock Desert, Nevada. Its 100,000 bhp jet engines propelled the driver, Andy Green, to more than 997 km/h to make it the world's first supersonic land speed record.

Extreme aircraft

All manner of aircraft make ideal subjects to draw in extreme perspective. Bold, distorted angles can be particularly effective in accentuating the blistering speed of these craft in flight.

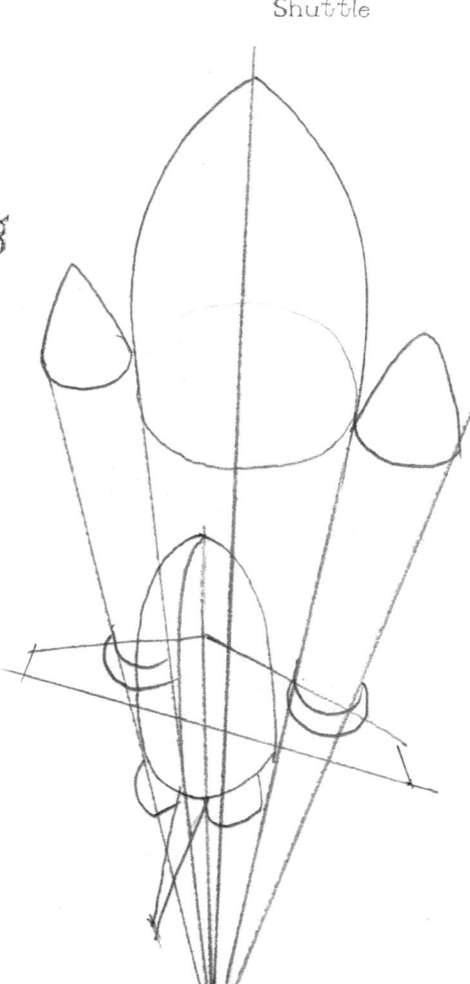

NASA Space Shuttle

High eye-level drawing

Draw guidelines to the vanishing point at the bottom and then sketch in the basic outline of the rocket and the shuttle attached to it.

Add further details to the outside of the shuttle and rocket, as well as the fire billowing from beneath it as it launches.

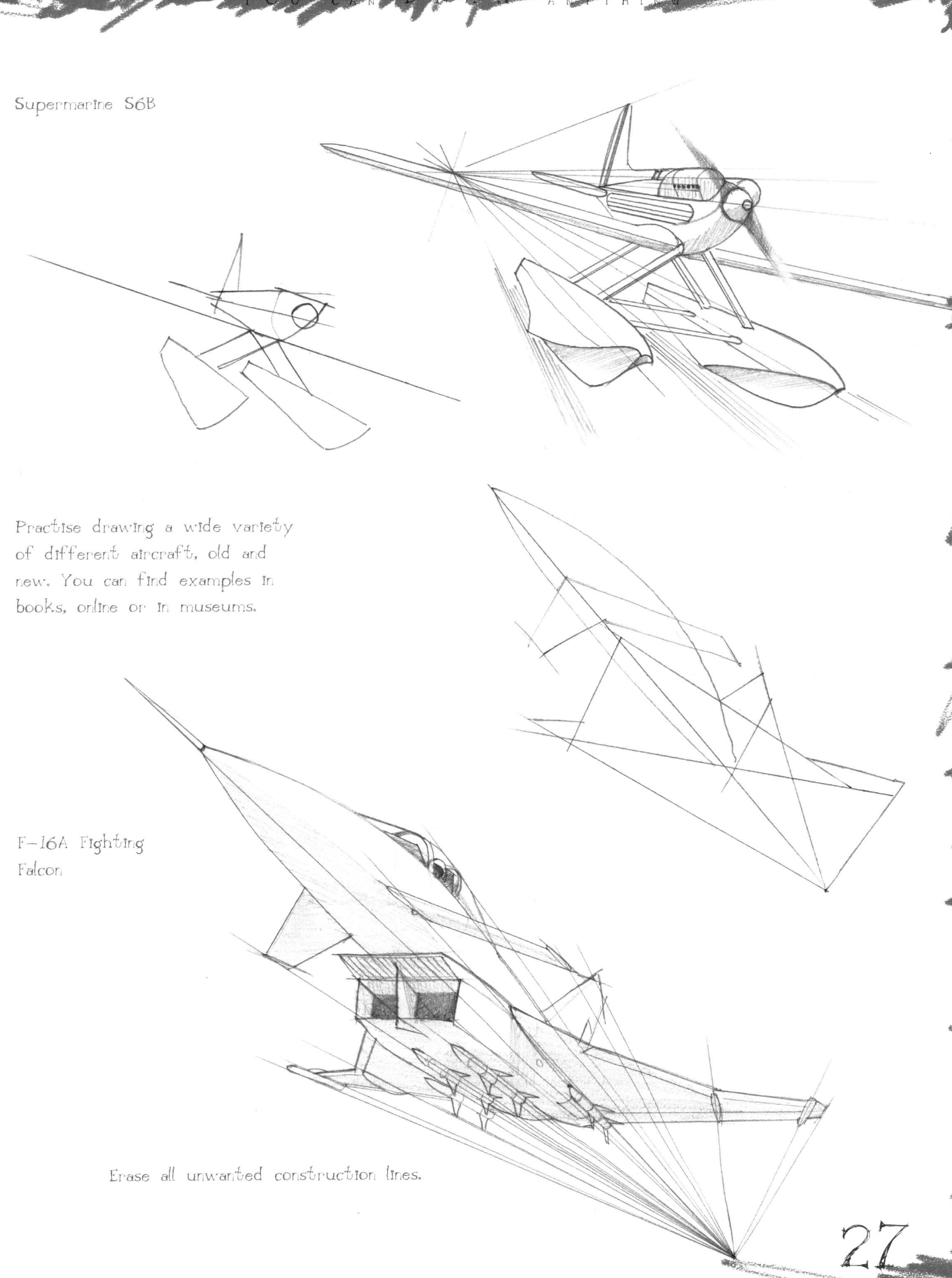

Supermarine S6B

Practise drawing a wide variety of different aircraft, old and new. You can find examples in books, online or in museums.

F-16A Fighting Falcon

Erase all unwanted construction lines.

Extreme cycling

Bicycles were first invented in the 19th century. There are now believed to be around 1 billion bicycles in the world. As they are found everywhere, cyclists make an easy subject to observe and practise drawing in perspective.

Practise doing quick sketches of cyclists: observe the different positions adopted for cycling on flat ground or uphill.

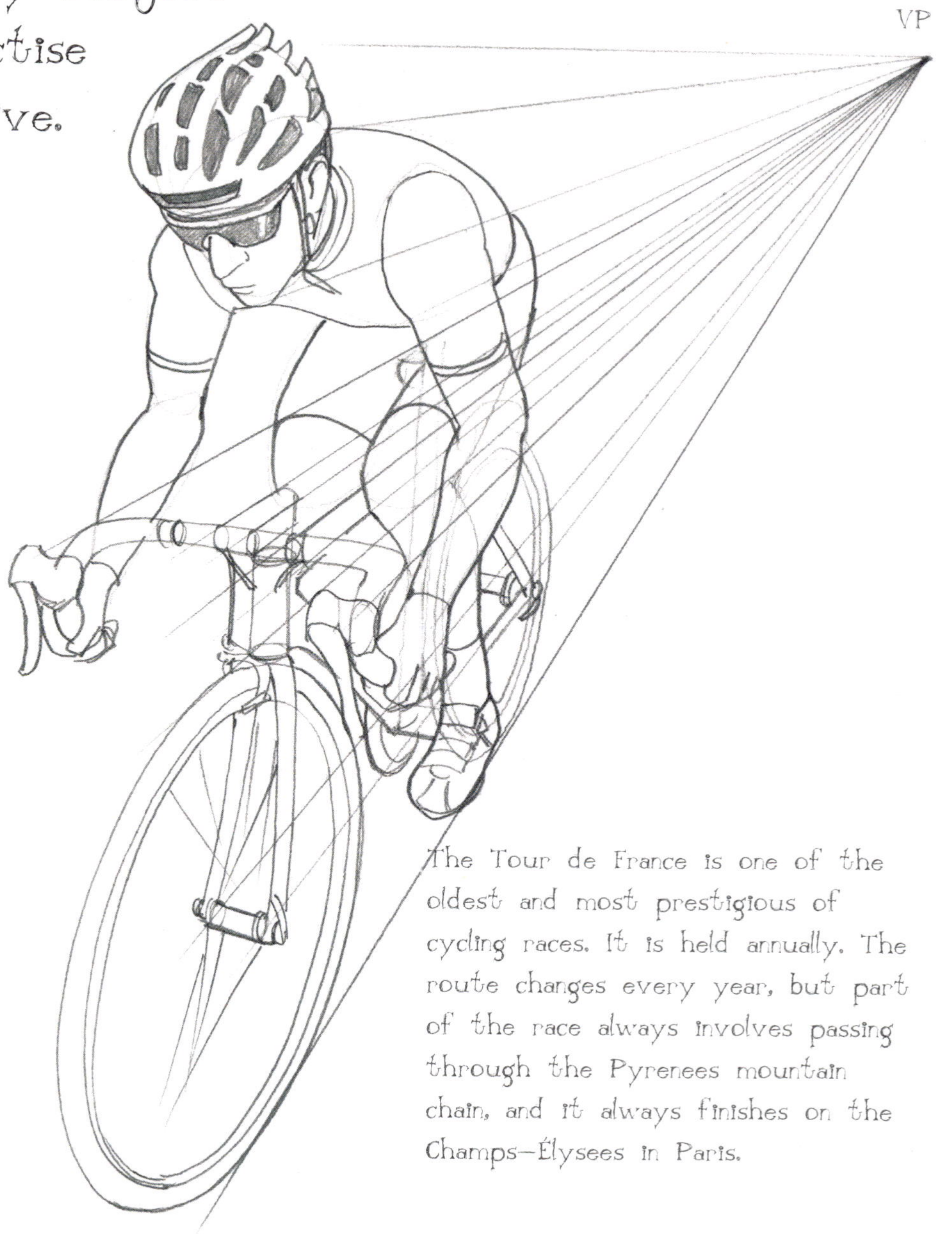

VP

The Tour de France is one of the oldest and most prestigious of cycling races. It is held annually. The route changes every year, but part of the race always involves passing through the Pyrenees mountain chain, and it always finishes on the Champs–Élysees in Paris.

This extreme perspective drawing shows a cyclist riding away from the viewer towards the vanishing point. This viewpoint creates a sense of depth that accentuates the main aspects of the sport – distance and speed.

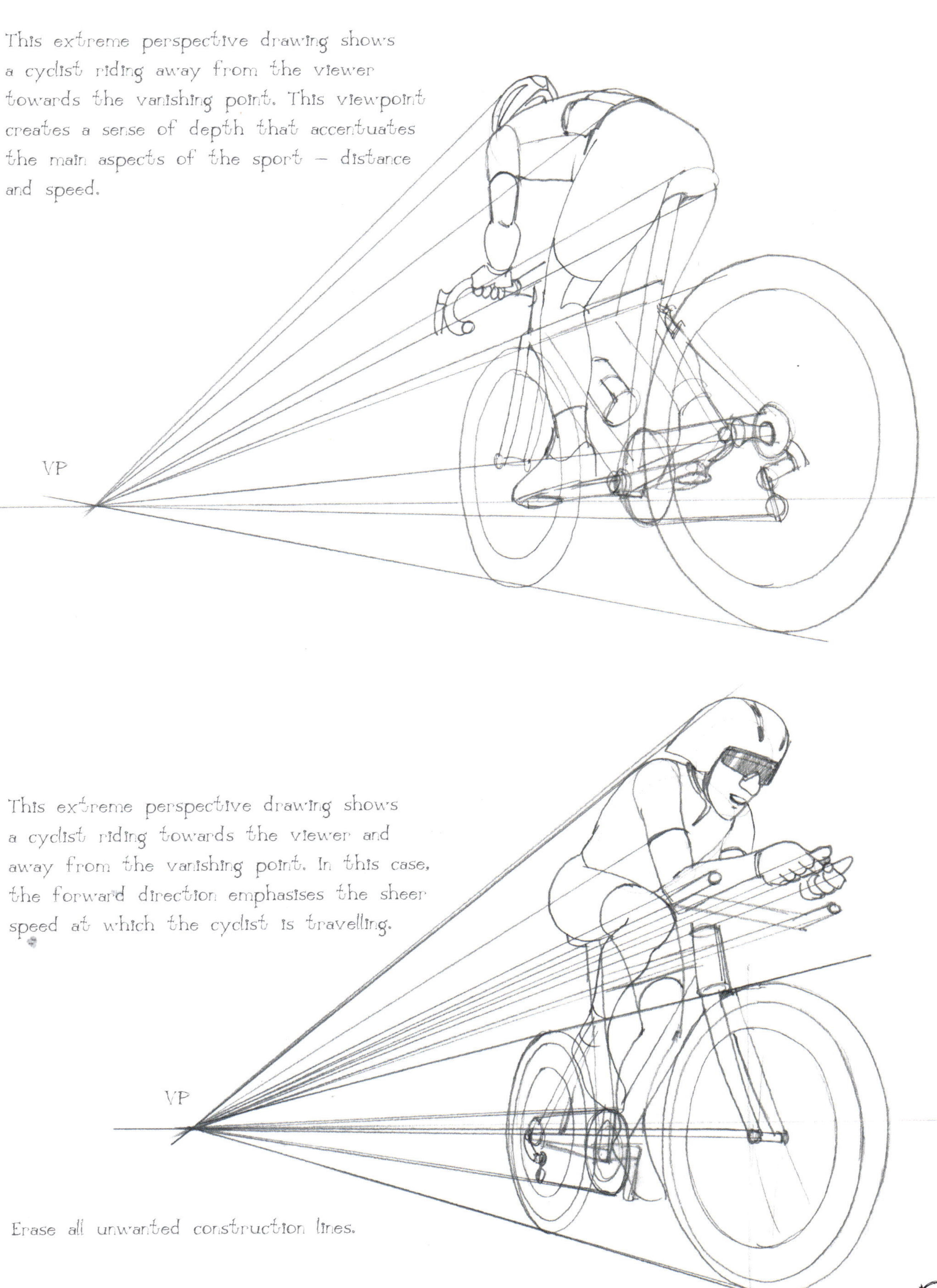

This extreme perspective drawing shows a cyclist riding towards the viewer and away from the vanishing point. In this case, the forward direction emphasises the sheer speed at which the cyclist is travelling.

Erase all unwanted construction lines.

Extreme Boats

You can use perspective to add character to any kind of boat: a fearsome pirate galleon, a 'floating city' cruiseliner or a chic, streamlined speedboat.

Sails are large pieces of fabric that catch the wind to propel a boat or ship forward. The shape of a sail changes depending on how the wind catches it.

Topsail schooner

A topsail schooner is a fairly large sailing vessel used to transport cargo.

High eye-level drawing.

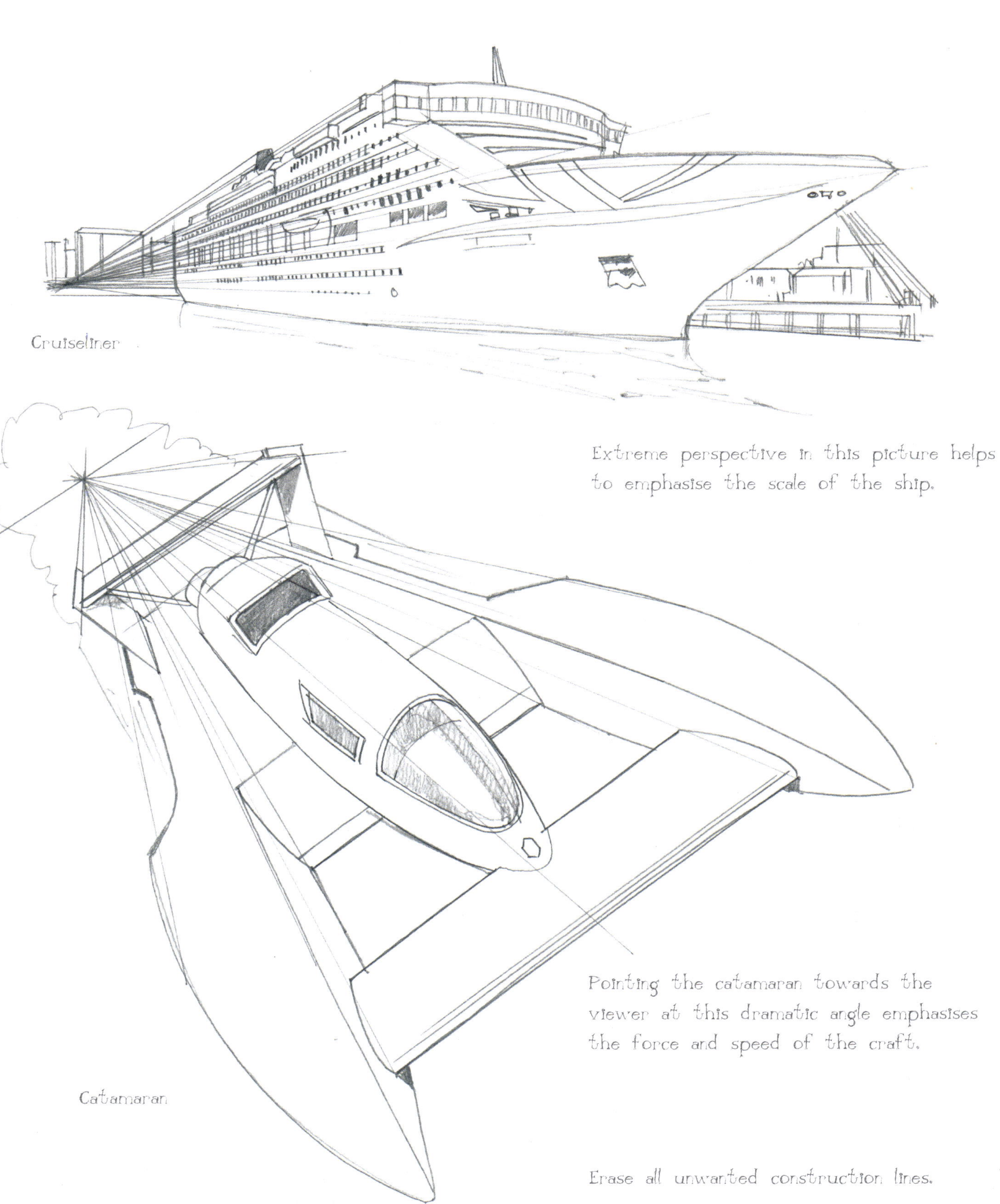

Cruiseliner

Extreme perspective in this picture helps to emphasise the scale of the ship.

Pointing the catamaran towards the viewer at this dramatic angle emphasises the force and speed of the craft.

Catamaran

Erase all unwanted construction lines.

Glossary

Composition The arrangement of the parts of a picture on the drawing paper.

Construction lines Guidelines used in the early stages of a drawing; they may be erased later.

Light source The direction from which the light seems to come in a drawing.

Proportion The correct relationship of scale between each part of the drawing.

Silhouette A drawing that shows only a flat dark shape, like a shadow.

Index